A TREE IS
GROWING

by ARTHUR DORROS
illustrated by S. D. SCHINDLER

SCHOLASTIC PRESS / New York

Library of Congress Cataloging-in-Publication Data

Dorros, Arthur.
A tree is growing / by Arthur Dorros; illustrated by S. D. Schindler. p. cm.
Summary: Tells about the structure of trees and how they grow, as well as their uses.
ISBN 0-590-45300-9
1. Trees — Growth — Juvenile literature. 2. Trees — Juvenile literature.
[1. Trees.] I. Schindler, S.D. ill. II. Title.
QK731.D67 1997
582.16 — dc20   96-10844   CIP   AC

12 11 10 9 8 7 6 5 4 3 2   7 8 9/9 0 1 2/0

Printed in the United States of America   37
First printing, April 1997

The illustrations were etched with a stylus and filled with
colored pencil on parchment and pastel papers.

The text type was set in Garamond.

Pictured on the back jacket are
Striped maple leaves and flowers.

Book design by Kristina Iulo

Special thanks to Gregory J. Waters,
botanist, horticulturist, and Director of Highstead Arboretum,
Redding, Connecticut, for his expert advice on trees.

To Sam, Sidney, Harriet and Sandy,
and the rest of my family tree

A.D.

🍃

To Phoebe Yeh and Kristina Iulo

S.D.S.

A giant tree may look as if it has always been big. But even the biggest tree keeps growing and changing. In the spring you can see that a tree is growing as you watch buds on the branches unfold into leaves.

White oak

Bristlecone pines are the oldest known living trees on earth. Some have been growing for five thousand years — since before the pyramids in Egypt were built.

With help from sunlight, leaves use tiny particles of gas from the air, and water from the ground, to make a kind of sugar. People breathe in oxygen and breathe out carbon dioxide gases. Tree leaves "breathe in" carbon dioxide gas from people, cars, and smoke, and release to the air oxygen that people need.

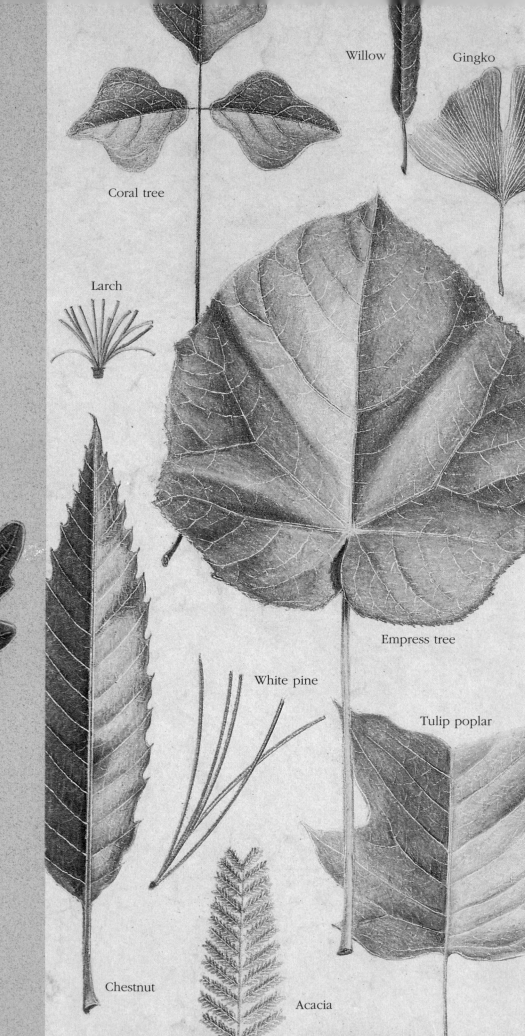

Sunlight

Carbon dioxide

Sugar

Oxygen

Water

Water

This process is called *photosynthesis.*

Coral tree

Willow

Gingko

Larch

Empress tree

White pine

Tulip poplar

Chestnut

Acacia

White oak

Palm

Leaves can be skinny needles or big heart shapes.
Whatever shape or size a leaf is, it makes food for the tree.
A kind of sugar is made in the leaves. Trees use the
sugar as food.

Orchid tree

Breadfruit
tree

Eucalyptus

Horse
chestnut

Red maple

The sugary water made in the leaves is mixed with other tree juices called sap. The food in the sap is carried throughout the tree. Where a branch breaks or where bark is cut, sap oozes out of a tree. The strong smells of some saps can keep insects from eating the trees they live on.

White pine

Large
wood nymph
butterfly

If you rub a sassafras leaf, the sap smells spicy.

Maple syrup is the boiled sap of sugar maple trees.

Baobab trees store water in the trunks. When a baobab tree trunk is swollen with water, it is round and fat. In dry weather, the tree gets water from the trunk. Then the trunk gets thinner.

Moth
caterpillar

Water

A tree needs sunlight, air, soil, and water to grow. Water travels through passages in the trunk and branches up to the leaves. The water moves up the trunk as if it is being sucked through a straw.

Sugary sap made in the leaves travels down other passages in the trunk, taking food to different parts of the tree.

A few kinds of trees drop roots from branches into the soil to gather water. Banyan tree roots grow into columns all around the tree.

White oak

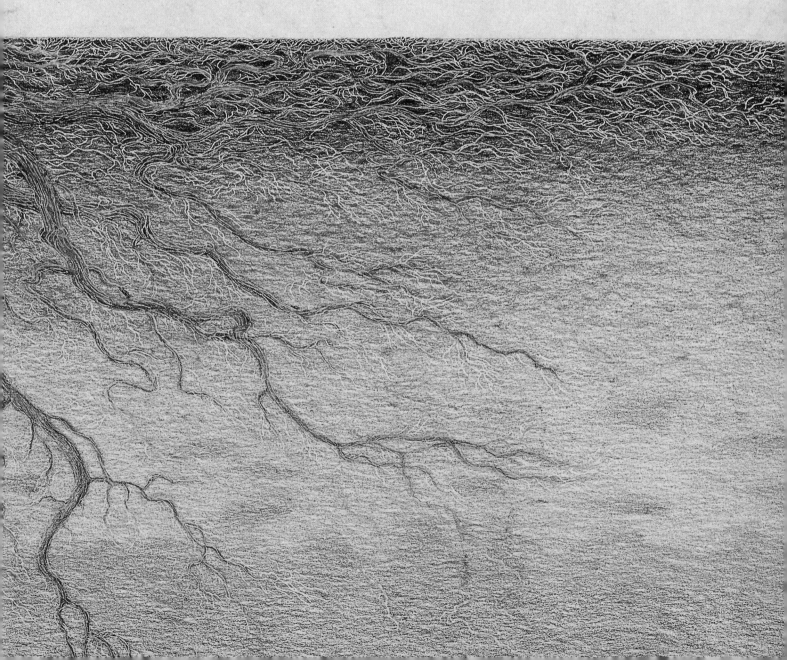

The roots of a tree grow into the ground and hold the tree in place. Roots are like pipelines. They absorb water and carry it into the tree.

A tree's roots spread out far underground. They usually grow out a little farther than the tree's branches.

Trees need minerals to grow. Minerals are tiny particles that are found in the soil. Salt is one kind of mineral. Like salt, other minerals dissolve in water. They are mixed in with the water that roots absorb and are carried throughout the tree.

Mushrooms growing among the roots of a tree can help it get minerals. And the mushrooms and plants growing near a tree get water brought by the tree's roots.

Cinnabar-red chanterelle mushrooms

Bicolored boletus mushrooms

Earthworms

Beetle grub

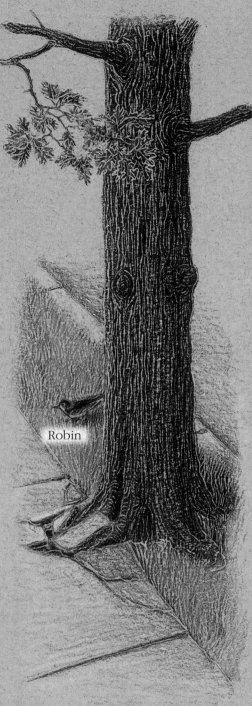

Robin

Growing roots are strong. A root can lift a sidewalk or split a rock as it grows. By splitting the rock, it helps make soil.

Flicker

Bark is the skin of a tree. The outer layer of bark protects the tree. When an oak tree is young, the bark is as smooth as a baby's skin. As the tree grows older, the bark becomes rough and cracked.

Polyphemus
moth

Looking at the bark
of a tree can help
you know what kind
of tree it is.

The cork used for
bulletin boards is the
peeled-off outer bark
of a cork oak tree.

Honey locust bark
has spines to help
protect the tree.

In cool climates,
cambium only grows
in spring and summer.
Count growth rings to see
how old a tree was when
it died. An old fir tree
can have over a
thousand rings, one
for each year it lived.

In tropical rain forest
trees, the cambium grows
all year and there are no
rings. It is hard to tell the
ages of those trees.

Growth rings

Snail

Phloem

Cambium

Xylem

Underwing moth

The bark you can touch and see is not growing anymore. Underneath it is a layer of growing bark, called *cambium*. Each year's cambium growth is a ring in the wood of a tree. As trees add new cambium, the trees become bigger around.

Next to the cambium are two layers called *xylem* and *phloem*. Water from the roots moves through the xylem, and sap from the leaves moves through the phloem.

Trees grow bigger around, and they grow taller.
As a tree grows, lower branches may fall off, making the
trunk look longer. But the branches do not move upward
on the trunk. A tree grows taller only at the top, as the
tips of the top branches grow upward.

If you find a mark on a tree trunk today, that mark
would stay at the same height for as long as the tree lives.

10 years

20 years

30 years

Wild turkey

50 years

200 years

Sequoias are some of the tallest trees in the world — over three hundred feet tall.

Nectar-eating
bat

Calabash tree

Catkin

Purple finch
(male)

Saucer
magnolia

*Birds, insects, and even
bats are attracted to
flowers to drink their
sweet juices. When
they brush the flowers,
the animals get a
powder called pollen on
them. The animals carry
the pollen to other
flowers. When the pollen
mixes with certain parts
of the flowers, seeds
grow. Wind also helps
pollinate flowers.*

In the spring, you can smell tree flowers. Tree flowers are found in many shapes and colors, and have many different smells. Parts of the flowers grow to become seeds. Oak trees have dangling clumps of flowers called catkins that help make acorns, the seeds of an oak tree.

Honey bee

Wild cherry

Purple finch (female)

Sugar maple

An oak tree can drop more than fifty thousand acorns in one year. Only a few of them grow into oak trees. Most are eaten, crushed, rot, or land in a place where they cannot take root.

Acorns can be carried away and dropped or buried by animals to grow in new places. Other kinds of seeds blow in the wind or float on water.

Sugar maple
seed

Acorns

Gray
squirrel

*Different kinds of
trees make seeds with
different coverings.
Nuts, cones, and fruits
all have seeds inside.*

Brazil nut

Mountain
pine cone

Cherry

*Coconuts are seeds of
a palm tree. A coconut
can float across the
ocean and sprout on
a sandy beach.*

*Autumn is a great time
to collect leaves.
Each tree has its own
special color.*

Tulip poplar

Gingko

Big-tooth
aspen

Sweet
gum

Pin oak

Titmouse

Sugar maple

White oak

Nuthatch

In cool climates, trees stop growing in autumn. The leaves of many trees stop making sugary food for the tree, and they lose their green color. Then you can see the red, brown, yellow, and orange colors that are also in the leaves.

Pine trees and some other trees have needles or leaves that do not change color in autumn.

Sow bugs

Mole

Centipede

When leaves fall to the ground, insects and worms eat them. The chewed and eaten bits of leaves make the soil better for growing trees and other plants.

In one small spoonful of soil, there can be hundreds of strange-looking living things that eat the fallen leaves. Many of the animals are too tiny to see, except with a microscope.

Common laccaria mushrooms

Springtails

Nematodes

Mites

Fungus

Spider

Earthworms

Beetles

Millipedes

Bacteria

Screech owl

Dogwood

White oak

Trees rest in the cold of winter, and their branches are bare. They may look as if they are dead. But look closely and you can see small buds that will become leaves and flowers in the spring.

Horse chestnut

In the spring, listen to the wind rustling
the leaves.
The trees are growing again.

White oak